Joey Goat

Barbara deRubertis
Illustrated by Jan Pyk

The Kane Press
New York

Library of Congress Cataloging-in-Publication Data

DeRubertis, Barbara.
Joey Goat/Barbara deRubertis; illustrated by Jan Pyk.
p.   cm.
"A Let's read together book."

Summary: Joey Goat loves to play tricks on his animal friends, but finally he learns
that a joke is only fun if everyone enjoys it.
ISBN 1-57565-025-8 (pbk.: alk. paper)
[1. Goats--Fiction.   2. Animals--Fiction.   3. Practical jokes--Fiction.   4. Stories in
rhyme.]
I. Pyk, Jan, 1934-   ill. II. Title.
PZ8.3.D455Jo 1997   96-6564
[E]--dc21   CIP
                                             AC

10 9 8 7 6 5 4

First published in the United States of America in 1997 by The Kane Press.
Printed in China.

Joey Goat
goes up the slope.
"Will Toby Toad
be home? I hope!

3

"I want to play
a little joke
on Toby Toad.
How he will croak!"

4

Joey opens
Toby's door.
He tiptoes in,
across the floor.

Toby snoozes.
Toby snores.
Joey pounces.
Joey ROARS!

Toby bolts
out of his bed.
Oh, what a jolt!
He bumps his head.

Joey Goat
rolls on the floor.
"I love a joke!
I must do more!"

Toby groans,
"Please don't do more.
That was no joke.
My head is sore!"

9

Joey says,
"I'm on my way.
I must go find
more jokes to play!"

Joey sees
a little hole.
It is the home
of Rosie Mole.

"What joke can I
play on a mole?
I know! I'll hide
her fishing pole!

"I'll hide it here,
by this old oak.
Oh, Rosie will just
love my joke."

Joey says,
"Now I'll go home.
And I'll call Rosie
on the phone.

"Rosie? This is
Joey Goat.
Shall we go fishing
in my boat?"

14

Rosie says,
"I'll get my pole.
I'll meet you at
the fishing hole."

15

Joey strolls
down to the hole.
And there he finds
poor Rosie Mole.

Rosie sobs,
"Boo hoo! Boo hoo!
Oh, Joey! I can't
fish with you!

"Someone stole
my fishing pole!
I am a MOST
unhappy mole."

Joey laughs
so hard he chokes.
"I am so good
at playing jokes!

"I hid your pole
behind the oak!"
Now Rosie frowns.
That's NOT a joke.

Poor Joey Goat.
He does not know
that Tony Crow
sees ALL below.

Tony softly
soars away.
"I have some chores
to do today."

The next day Joey
hears "Hello!"
He turns around.
It's Tony Crow.

Tony says, "Please
come! Please do!
I have a joke
that's just for you.

"We'll cross this bridge.
Now follow me.
This joke's the best
you'll ever see."

Joey wonders
what's in store.
A TROLL! It makes
a horrid ROAR.

Slowly, Joey
turns around.
ANOTHER troll!
A horrid sound!

Joey cries,
"Oh, woe is me!"
He sobs and chokes.
"Please set me free!"

Tony Crow says,
"That will do.
Now take a look.
This joke's on you!"

Joey groans.
Those are not trolls!
They're only MASKS
of trolls—on poles!

And who is holding
up each pole?
It's Toby Toad!
And Rosie Mole!

"I've learned my lesson,"
Joey chokes.
"I am so sorry
for my jokes.

"I see that jokes
are only fun
when they are fun
for *everyone!*"